MIND-BLOWING SCIENCE EXPERIMENTS

MAGNIFICENT EXPERIMENTS WITH MATERIALS

Thomas Canavan

Gareth Stevens
PUBLISHING

Please visit our website, www.garethstevens.com.
For a free color catalog of all our high-quality books,
call toll free 1-800-542-2595 or fax 1-877-542-2596.

Cataloging-in-Publication Data

Names: Canavan, Thomas.
Title: Magnificent experiments with materials / Thomas Canavan.
Description: New York : Gareth Stevens Publishing, 2018. | Series: Mind-blowing science experiments | Includes index.
Identifiers: ISBN 9781538207482 (pbk.) | ISBN 9781538207444 (library bound) | ISBN 9781538207321 (6 pack)
Subjects: LCSH: Matter--Properties--Experiments--Juvenile literature. | Materials--Experiments--Juvenile literature. |
    Science--Experiments--Juvenile literature.
Classification: LCC QC173.36 C317 2018 | DDC 530.4078--dc23

Published in 2018 by
Gareth Stevens Publishing
111 East 14th Street, Suite 349
New York, NY 10003

Copyright © Arcturus Holdings Limited

Author: Thomas Canavan
Illustrator: Adam Linley
Experiments Coordinator: Anna Middleton
Designer: Elaine Wilkinson
Designer series edition: Emma Randall
Editors: Joe Harris, Rebecca Clunes, Frances Evans

All images courtesy of Shutterstock.

Printed in China
CPSIA compliance information: Batch CS17GS: For further information contact
Gareth Stevens, New York, New York at 1-800-542-2595.

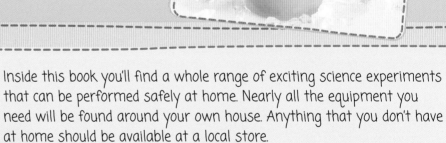

Having Fun and Being Safe

Inside this book you'll find a whole range of exciting science experiments that can be performed safely at home. Nearly all the equipment you need will be found around your own house. Anything that you don't have at home should be available at a local store.

We have given some recommendations alongside the instructions to let you know when adult help might be needed. However, the degree of adult supervision will vary, depending on the age of the reader and the experiment. We would recommend close adult supervision for any experiment involving cooking equipment, sharp implements, electrical equipment, or batteries.

The author and publisher cannot take responsibility for any injury, damage, or mess that might occur as a result of attempting the experiments in this book. Always tell an adult before you perform any experiments, and follow the instructions carefully.

Contents

Lava Lamp 4

Citrus Candle 6

The Burning Rope Trick 8

Heavy Weather... 11

The Pushy Candle 14

Getting Fizzy-cal 16

Paper That Won't Budge..................................... 18

The Carbon Dragon 20

Vinegar Rocket...22

Plastic Milk? 24

Stepping on Eggshells...26

Water from the Sun...28

Glossary & Further Information 31

Index 32

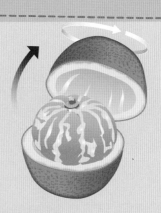

A note about measurements

Measurements are given in U.S. form with metric in parentheses. The metric conversion is rounded to make it easier to measure.

Have you ever made something just disappear, or conjured something out of nothing? You might manage both of these tricks with these experiments!

Lava Lamp

- Tall, clear drinking glass
- Water
- Cooking oil
- Salt shaker
- Food coloring

If there's anyone in your family who can remember the 1970s, they can tell you about lava lamps. These fun lamps were clear tubes with colorful "lava" blobs that constantly bobbed up and down. You can make your own groovy version with this experiment!

1

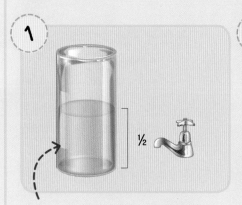

Fill the glass halfway with water.

2

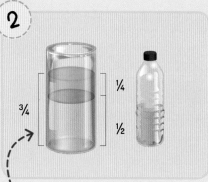

Slowly pour oil into the glass until it is about ¾ full.

3

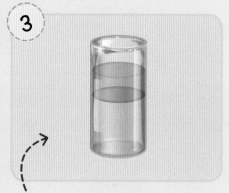

Wait until the **liquids** settle. They will form two layers — the oil on top and water below.

4

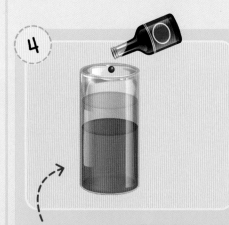

Add a few drops of food coloring. They will pass through the oil, but will change the color of the water.

5

Shake some salt into the glass and wait a few seconds.

6

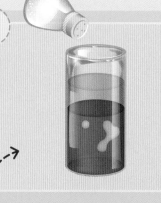

Blobs of oil will sink to the bottom of the glass, then float back up from the water layer.

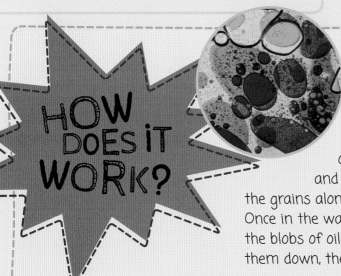

HOW DOES IT WORK?

Oil is less dense than water, which means the same amount of it weighs less. This is why the oil floats on the water's surface. Food coloring is water-based, so it sinks through the oil. Salt is denser than oil, so the grains of salt sink through the oil and down into the water. But some oil sticks to the grains along the way, and the oil goes along for the ride. Once in the water, though, the salt dissolves. That leaves the blobs of oil on their own. Without the salt to weigh them down, they float back up to the oil layer.

TOP TIP!
If the effect slows down or stops, just add a little more salt.

WHAT HAPPENS IF...?

Supermarkets stock many different types of cooking oil. You could try this experiment several times, using a different type of oil each time, such as sunflower oil, rapeseed oil, or olive oil. Based on the results, can you judge which of the oils has the highest **density**?

REAL-LIFE SCIENCE

The original lava lamps were clear tubes filled with liquid and blobs of colored wax that settled at the bottom. A bright light beneath the tube would warm the wax, making it less dense. Blobs of this less-dense wax would rise up through the liquid, then cool down, become denser, and sink to the bottom of the tube again.

Citrus Candle

You've probably smelled fruit-scented candles before, but have you ever heard of a candle made from real fruit? In this experiment, you can use an orange—and some scientific knowledge—to make the ultimate citrus candle!

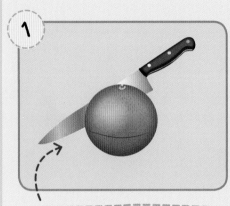

1 Ask an adult to cut into an orange horizontally, with the stalk on top. They should slice all the way around the middle of the orange, cutting no deeper than the skin.

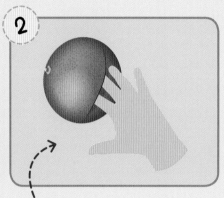

2 Carefully slide your fingers under the orange's skin. Work your way around the orange.

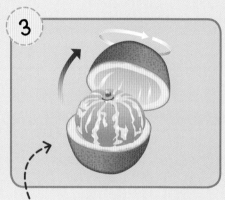

3 Twist the two halves slightly as you carefully pull them apart.

4 Put the half that doesn't contain the orange flesh to one side. Carefully remove the flesh from the other half, making sure you don't pull out the stalk.

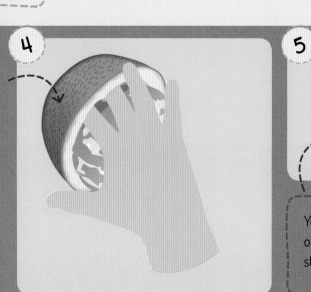

5 You should now have an empty orange half, with the stalk sticking up in the middle.

6

Slowly pour olive oil onto the stalk until it almost fills the emptied orange half.

7

Ask the adult to light the stalk with a match and turn off the lights in the room. Enjoy your citrus candle!

WHAT HAPPENS IF...?

Try this experiment again following all the instructions until you reach step 6. This time, don't pour the olive oil onto the stalk. Instead, pour it directly into the orange's skin. Do you think the stalk will burn more quickly, more slowly, or not at all? Ask an adult to light the stalk to find out.

REAL-LiFE SCiENCE

The olive oil in this candle moves up the stalk towards the flame, just like melted wax on a regular candle. This movement of liquid is called capillary action, and plants get water from their roots in the same way. The tiniest blood vessels in your body are called capillaries, and they move blood back and forth with the help of capillary action, too.

Any type of candle works by burning a fuel, which warms until it becomes a **gas**, or **vapor**. A gas is a state of matter that is usually reached when a material is warmed up. The material begins in a different state—such as a **solid** or liquid—and becomes a gas when it is heated. The olive oil was the fuel in this candle, going from liquid to gas as the candle burned. The wax in a normal candle goes from solid to gas, although sometimes you see a bit that's melted.

The Burning Rope Trick

Magicians sometimes do funny tricks with rope. They can make rope rise up or even dance. You can try a mini magic trick with thread that should produce some gasps from your audience! How does lighting a rope on fire without it burning away sound?

YOU WILL NEED

- Ruler
- 2 kitchen chairs
- Light wooden curtain ring, about 1½ inches (4 cm) wide
- Matches and an adult to help you
- Scissors
- Teaspoon
- Cereal bowl
- Salt
- Warm water

1

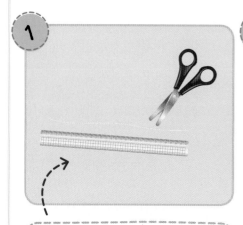

Cut a length of thread about 18 inches (45 cm) long.

2

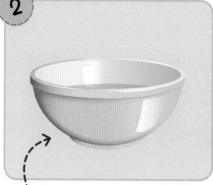

Fill the bowl halfway with warm water.

3

Add 4 teaspoons of salt and stir.

4

Put the thread in the bowl and let it soak for a minute, then let it dry.

5

Repeat step 4 three more times.

6

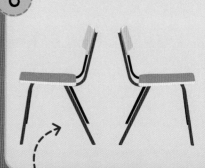

Set the chairs up back-to-back, with about a 6-inch (15 cm) gap between the tops of the chairs.

7

Place the ruler so that it spans the gap between the chairs.

8

Tie one end of the thread to the curtain ring and the other around the middle of the ruler. The curtain ring will now hang between the chairs.

9

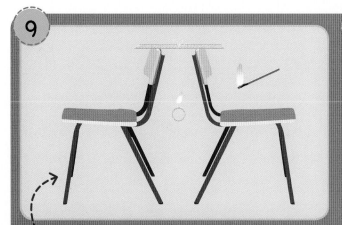

Ask an adult to light the thread just above the ring.

10

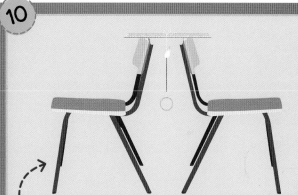

The flame will move up the thread, leaving a thin column of ash behind — but the ring will still be held up!

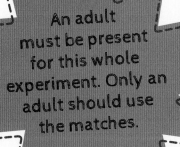

An adult must be present for this whole experiment. Only an adult should use the matches.

TOP TIP!

Be very patient when soaking and drying the thread.

Continued

HOW DOES IT WORK?

The key to this experiment is the salt, which dissolved in the water. The thread soaks up some of that salt solution. When you dry the thread, the water evaporates and leaves the salt behind. If the solution is very salt-heavy, the salt can form crystals as the thread is dried. The magic? Well, that's because the salt crystals burn at a higher temperature than the cotton thread! The string is now a thin column of salt, and the thread has burned away!

WHAT HAPPENS IF...?

The trick is to make sure the string soaks up enough of the salt solution. You also need to make sure the solution is salty enough. Try repeating this experiment with different amounts of salt to find out exactly how much salt is needed. Start with a small amount. If the ring falls, keep adding more salt until it works.

REAL-LIFE SCIENCE

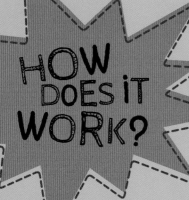

Maybe you have "sea salt" in your kitchen. It's basically salt water, but without the water. In some flat, coastal areas, each tide delivers a layer of water, which rests in shallow puddles on hard ground. As the tide recedes, and the Sun beats down, the water evaporates and the sea salt is raked up for collection.

Heavy Weather

Barometers measure **air pressure**, which helps **predict** the weather. They are some of the most sensitive scientific instruments. They can be very complex in their setup, but you can make your very own with just a few household items!

YOU WILL NEED

- Drinking glass
- Balloon
- Scissors
- Plastic drinking straw
- String
- Modeling clay
- Paper and pencil
- Tape
- Table by a wall
- A friend would come in handy

1

Cut a piece of balloon in the shape of a circle, about 2 inches (5 cm) wider than the mouth of the glass.

2

Stretch that piece across the mouth, holding it tightly in place just below the rim.

3

Tie the string around the glass, keeping the rubber stretched tightly across the top. You may need your friend's help.

4

Form a piece of modeling clay about the size of a large pea and roll it to get it soft.

5

Place this modeling clay on the center of the stretched balloon rubber.

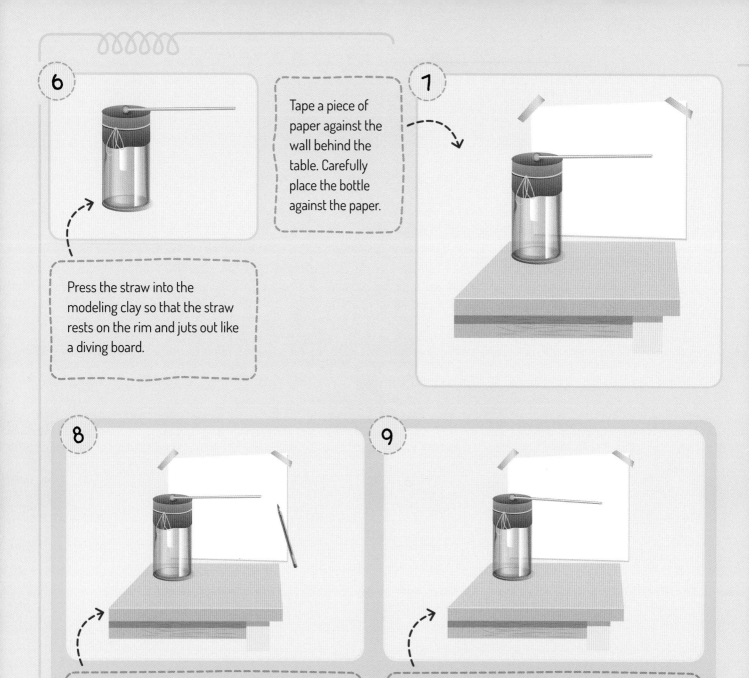

6

Press the straw into the modeling clay so that the straw rests on the rim and juts out like a diving board.

Tape a piece of paper against the wall behind the table. Carefully place the bottle against the paper.

7

8

Mark the paper to show the level of the straw, noting the date.

9

Repeat step 8 every day for a week. The level should go up and down slightly, depending on the weather.

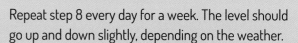

TOP TIP!

Make sure to do this experiment away from direct sunlight and any other source of heat. Heat will affect the way the straw moves, and you want the results to show changes in air pressure only.

HOW DOES IT WORK?

You've just done an experiment that deals with one of the main states of matter—gas. Air is a mixture of gases and, like any gas, it can change shape and **volume**. You've probably heard of compressed air. That's simply air that has been "pressed" into a smaller volume. Changing weather is usually a result of changing air pressure. Nice weather usually accompanies high pressure. In your experiment, the higher the air pressure, the more the air pushes down on the rubber seal and squeezes the air inside. With the rubber moving down, the far end of the straw goes up — like a seesaw. Your markings should show the rise and fall of air pressure as the weather changes.

WHAT HAPPENS IF...?

Try to predict what would happen if you used a different material to cover the mouth of the glass, like Saran wrap or cooking foil. What are the qualities of the balloon rubber that might make it behave differently? Test and observe.

REAL-LIFE SCIENCE

Monitoring air pressure is one of the most important features of weather forecasting. You'll hear forecasters predicting rain if there is a low-pressure front coming in, or predicting pleasant weather when the air pressure is high. Forecasters use highly sensitive barometers, which can pick up the slightest changes in air pressure.

the Pushy Candle

YOU WILL NEED

- Plastic tray
- Drinking glass
- Water
- Matches
- Candle
- Two small paperback books

A candle flame can do all sorts of things—light a room, provide warmth, or create a feeling of coziness. But can you imagine a candle pushing and shoving things around? If you know how to harness the right forces, you can see this for yourself!

1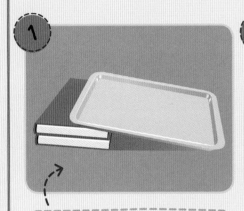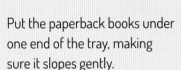

Put the paperback books under one end of the tray, making sure it slopes gently.

2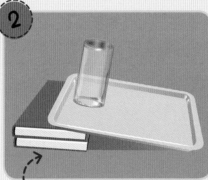

Wet the rim of the glass all around and set it upside down at the higher end of the tray.

3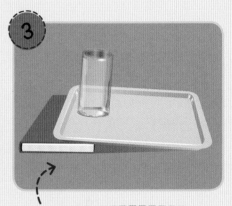

The glass should stay in position. If it begins to slide, remove one of the books.

4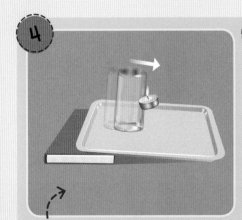

Ask an adult to light the candle and hold it close to the side of the glass without touching it.

5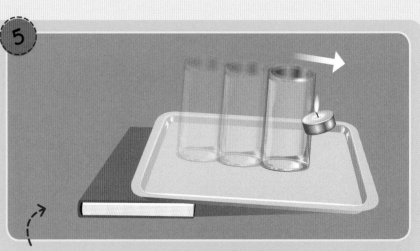

The glass will begin to glide mysteriously and smoothly down the slope of the tray. Make sure the adult follows the course of the glass, keeping the candle close to it.

HOW DOES IT WORK?

The floating glass traveled along on a cushion of air, which you helped to produce. The heat from the candle warmed the air inside the glass. The gases in the glass expanded as the temperature increased, pushing the glass up from the surface of the tray. This meant that the rim of the glass was no longer touching the tray itself—instead the rim was resting on the water. The surface tension of the water kept the rim in contact with the tray, so the heated air didn't escape from the glass. Without the **friction** of the glass touching the tray, the glass moved easily across the surface of the tray.

TOP TIP!

The candle can be held on any side of the glass, as long as it's close enough to warm the air inside.

WHAT HAPPENS IF...?

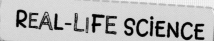

Remember that you need a gentle slope to make this experiment work at its best. If the tray is too level, the glass won't move, even though it will have the expanded air inside it. But if the tray slopes too much, the glass could tip over because it has become unstable.

REAL-LIFE SCIENCE

It's not just upside-down glasses that can travel on a cushion of air. Large vehicles called hovercrafts work on a similar principle. Powerful fans send air down below the hovercraft, allowing it to lift up off the water. Since it doesn't touch the water, the hovercraft has less friction than a boat. It can travel more quickly than standard ferries.

Getting Fizzy-Cal

When you think of laws, you might picture lawyers and judges. But laws don't just apply to people—everything in nature behaves according to laws that scientists have observed. Here's a law you can test yourself at home!

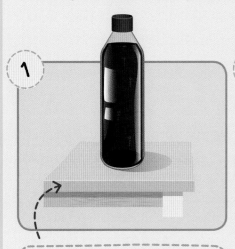

1 Keep the bottle steady and place it on a table or counter.

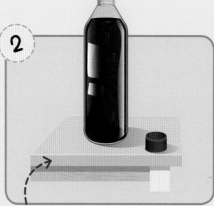

2 Slowly remove the lid.

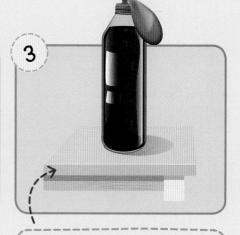

3 Slide the mouth of the balloon over the mouth of the bottle.

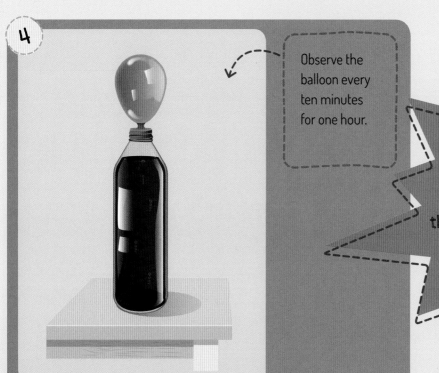

4 Observe the balloon every ten minutes for one hour.

You're on safe ground here, but just make sure you don't shake the bottle before opening it—it would ruin the experiment and make a mess.

HOW DOES IT WORK?

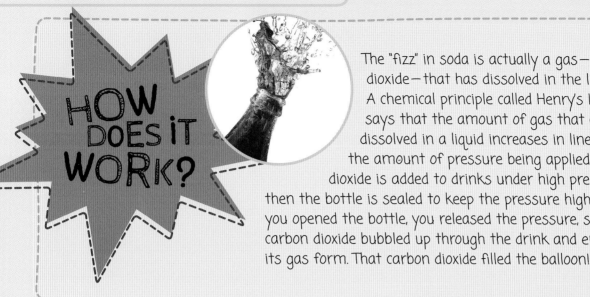

The "fizz" in soda is actually a gas—carbon dioxide—that has dissolved in the liquid. A chemical principle called Henry's Law says that the amount of gas that can be dissolved in a liquid increases in line with the amount of pressure being applied. Carbon dioxide is added to drinks under high pressure and then the bottle is sealed to keep the pressure high. When you opened the bottle, you released the pressure, so the carbon dioxide bubbled up through the drink and emerged in its gas form. That carbon dioxide filled the balloon!

TOP TIP!

You can do this experiment inside or out, but just make sure conditions aren't too windy if you're outside.

WHAT HAPPENS IF...?

The Internet has thousands of videos of people dropping mints into diet cola to create huge sprays of soda. That dramatic reaction is really a high-speed version of the release of carbon dioxide when you open a bottle of soda. When you look at these mints up close, you can see they have tiny bumps. The dissolved carbon dioxide latches onto these bumps and turns back into gas incredibly fast!

REAL-LIFE SCIENCE

Dissolved gases can be dangerous. Deep-sea divers need to return to the water's surface slowly, because the high pressure of deep water causes some of the gases they breathe in (from their tanks) to become dissolved in their blood. Coming up too fast and releasing that pressure quickly could cause the gases to bubble up in the blood.

17

Paper That Won't Budge

Imagine doing an experiment that demonstrates something special about fluids, all without getting wet or even using water! That's just one of the surprises in store for you here—another is how fast this experiment will go!

YOU WILL NEED

- A piece of printer paper
- A table
- Scissors
- A friend

1

Fold the paper in half so that the crease is halfway up the long side. Cut carefully along the crease. The two halves of paper should be equal in size.

2

Take one of the pieces and fold the right-hand edge ¼ of the way along the long side.

3

Ask a friend to blow the paper off the table. The paper should flatten against the table rather than blow away.

4

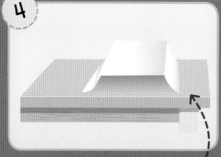

Unfold the flaps and stand the paper (like a bridge) on the table about 1 foot (30 cm) in from the edge.

5

Ask a friend to blow the paper off the table. The paper should flatten against the table rather than blow away.

HOW DOES IT WORK?

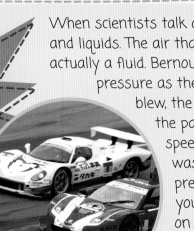

When scientists talk about fluids, they mean both gases and liquids. The air that your friend was blowing was actually a fluid. Bernoulli's Principle tells us that fluids lose pressure as they move faster. When your friend blew, the air **molecules** rushed quickly under the paper, losing pressure as they increased speed. So the air above the paper—which wasn't being blown and still had normal pressure—forced the paper down. Maybe you've seen racing cars with funny wings on their backs? They serve the same purpose—forcing the car downwards, so it doesn't fly off the track at high speeds!

WHAT HAPPENS IF...?

What would happen if your friend blew across and over the folded piece of paper? You can probably predict the answer. Can you think of any other folded shapes that would also "anchor" the paper? Try a few and find out why they work—or fail.

TOP TIPS!
Be careful when using scissors!

REAL-LIFE SCIENCE

Bernoulli's Principle lies behind lots of design. A plane's wing has an airfoil shape – the top is curved but the bottom is flat. That curve speeds up the air as it passes over the wing, but the slightly slower-moving air beneath has more pressure. That difference in pressure forces the wing—and the plane—upwards.

The Carbon Dragon

With just a bit of scientific trickery, you can turn an ordinary household rubber glove into a scary looking dragon. This is another experiment that looks like magic, but it depends on chemistry. You might have to choose between a magician's cape and a scientist's white coat!

YOU WILL NEED

- Lightweight rubber glove
- Vinegar
- Baking soda
- Tablespoon
- Felt-tip or marker pen
- Drinking glass (the glove should fit snugly around the rim)

1

Draw a scary dragon's face on the glove, using the fingers to show the dragon's horns and plumes of smoke.

2

Add 3 tablespoons of vinegar to the glass.

3

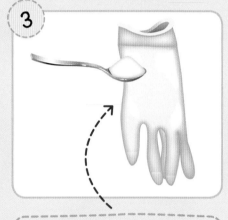

Hold the glove with the fingers pointing down. Sprinkle 2 tablespoons of baking soda into it. Make sure that it gets into the fingers.

4

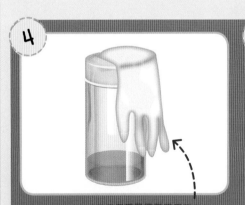

Keeping the glove floppy, with fingers pointing down, fit the wrist of the glove over the rim of the glass.

5

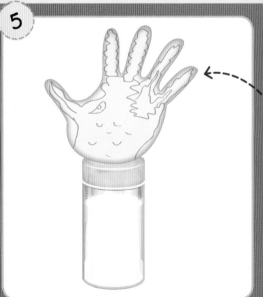

Lift the tips of the glove fingers upright so that the baking soda falls into the glass. Watch as the glove begins to inflate, growing larger and more upright. The dragon will get a new, terrifying look!

20

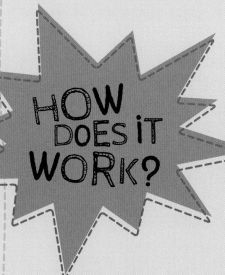

HOW DOES IT WORK?

You're examining more than one scientific effect with this experiment! You already know that combining different materials can produce a third. In this experiment, you have combined a liquid (vinegar) with a solid (baking soda) and produced a gas (carbon dioxide). It's the carbon dioxide that builds up thanks to the reaction, filling the flexible rubber glove and giving the face its scary character. This experiment also shows the importance of choosing the right material. Rubber can stretch, so the glove can blow up like a balloon and let your dragon come to life!

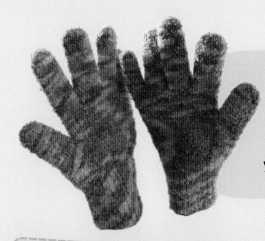

How would the experiment work if you used a glove made of wool instead of rubber? Make a prediction and record your findings.

WHAT HAPPENS IF...?

REAL-LIFE SCIENCE

Materials that behave in similar ways are often grouped together. Baking soda is part of a group known as bases, and they often react strongly with another group, known as acids. Vinegar contains acid, like many foods, especially citrus fruits such as oranges, lemons, and limes. This experiment would also work well with lemon juice instead of vinegar.

Vinegar Rocket

5, 4, 3, 2, 1…BLAST OFF! Gases, even invisible ones, can pack a real punch! You'll see that firsthand in this dramatic experiment. Ask an adult to help you and check out the "Top Tips" before you get started.

YOU WILL NEED

- Goggles
- Tablespoon
- Teaspoon
- Cylinder can with a snap-on lid
- Baking soda
- Vinegar
- Scissors
- Clear tape
- Card stock
- Ruler

1

Cut 3 right-angled triangles from the card stock. The shorter sides of each triangle should be about 1 inch (3 cm) long.

2

Fold one of those equal sides back about ½ inch (1 cm) on each triangle.

3

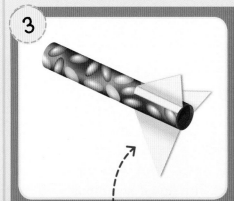

Turn the cylinder upside down so that it's resting on the lid. Tape the card stock triangles on to make three fins.

4

Turn the cylinder right-side up and remove the lid. Add 1 tablespoon of vinegar. Ask an adult to add ½ teaspoon of baking soda to the cylinder.

5

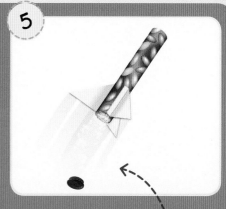

Click the lid back on and ask the adult to turn the cylinder upside down. It should now be standing on its lid. Stand back and wait 10 to 15 seconds for the rocket to take off!

HOW DOES IT WORK?

Your rocket blasted off because of the power of a gas (carbon dioxide) that you helped produce when the baking soda reacted with the acid contained in the vinegar. In fact, it's the speed of that reaction—how fast the carbon dioxide was produced—that packs the power. The amount of gas produced is far, far greater than the volume of the cylinder. So the gas pressed against the sides of the canister harder and harder as more of it was produced—then found the "weak spot," which was the lid. That's why the lid blew off like a rocket!

WHAT HAPPENS IF...?

What do you suppose would happen if you used water instead of vinegar and a fizzing vitamin tablet instead of baking soda? Grab an adult to help you and find out!

TOP TIPS!

- An adult (wearing goggles) should load the rocket and launch it.

- This project is messy! Do it outdoors.

- Wait at least a minute if the rocket doesn't launch before an adult checks on it.

REAL-LIFE SCIENCE

You experience a version of this experiment whenever you ride in a car. Small amounts of fuel are ignited by a car's spark plugs. The fuel turns into a gas, which pushes pistons, which in turn propel the car forwards. It all happens even faster in a racing car!

Plastic Milk?

Milk can turn into yogurt or cheese, but can it really turn into plastic? With just a little bit of help from you, it could pass for plastic! Ask an adult to help you with this experiment.

1

Pour 8 fluid ounces (250 ml) of milk into a saucepan and ask an adult to heat it slightly.

2

When the milk is hot but not boiling, ask an adult to take it off the heat. Stir in 4 teaspoons of vinegar.

3

Continue stirring for a minute.

4

Rest the sieve on the mixing bowl and pour the milk through it. White lumps should remain in the strainer after the liquid has gone through.

5

Dump the lumps onto the tray and let them cool for a few minutes. Press the lumps into a rubbery ball, or any shape you choose! Set it aside and in a day or two, it will harden into a tough plastic form.

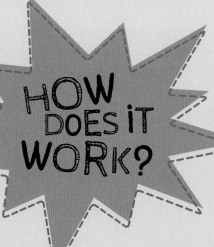

HOW DOES IT WORK?

Have you ever had heated milk in your hot cocoa or oatmeal? It never turns into rubber or plastic, even when it cools. The difference seems to be adding vinegar. That's where the chemistry kicks in, changing one familiar material (milk) into something that looks and feels like another (plastic). The vinegar contains an acid, which causes the milk to separate into a liquid, which poured through the sieve, and a solid made of fats and a protein called casein. This casein is made up of molecules that link up and behave like plastic molecules.

WHAT HAPPENS IF...?

It was the acid in the vinegar that kick-started this experiment. Why not try the experiment again with lemon juice (which also contains an acid), to see whether it would still work. Make a prediction and observe the results.

TOP TIPS!

You need an adult present at all times in this experiment. Only an adult should heat the milk on the stove.

REAL-LIFE SCIENCE

Casein, the key to the plastic side of this experiment, is used in lots of ways from making paints and glues to helping dentists make teeth stronger. Have you ever taken a bite of pizza and found a string of cheese that grew longer and longer? That happens because of the casein in the pizza's cheese topping!

Stepping on Eggshells

When you hear people say the phrase "walking on eggshells," you know they really mean, "being careful." Everyone knows eggshells break easily, but if you use a little science, you can get those shells to support a lot of weight. See for yourself!

YOU WILL NEED

- 4 eggs and some extras
- Clear tape
- Small, sharp scissors
- Several large, heavy books, such as telephone books
- Small mixing bowl
- Spoon

1

Over a bowl, tap the narrow end of each egg with a spoon until is cracks. Let the egg drip into the bowl. Remove any shell fragments. You could use the contents of this bowl for cooking later.

2

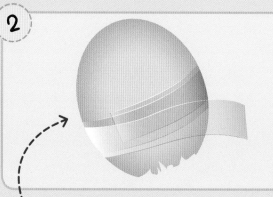

Carefully wind some tape around the widest part of each egg.

3

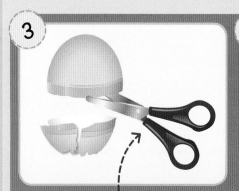

Use the scissors to cut around the middle of the tape to create four "egg domes" of equal size.

4

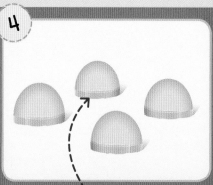

Lay the four egg domes on a counter or table, forming a rectangle.

5

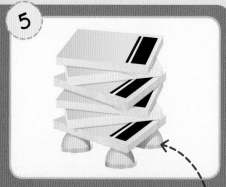

Slowly lay a book on the "egg rectangle." The shells won't break! See how many more books you can add until they finally give way.

HOW DOES IT WORK?

When a hen sits on its eggs, the narrow ends of the eggs are always pointing up. The hen could easily break the eggs otherwise. Eggs have one of the strongest designs possible—they're dome shaped. A dome is able to spread the pressure from above (like the weight of a hen) evenly through the entire structure. There's no single part of the dome that has more work to do than any other. This is why domes and arches (which also spread pressure) are important for architects designing large buildings.

WHAT HAPPENS IF...?

What if the eggshells are pointing sideways, not vertically? To find out, you need to pierce both ends of four eggs with a pin. Then probe inside with a wider toothpick, put a straw to one hole and gently blow the egg contents into a bowl. Lay the empty eggshells on their side in a rectangle pattern and repeat the experiment. Predict how many books you'll be able to stack this time!

TOP TIPS!

Ask an adult to help when you're cutting the shells.

REAL-LIFE SCIENCE

Some of the most beautiful buildings in the world—the Taj Mahal, St. Paul's Cathedral, the U.S. Capitol—have instantly recognizable domes. They look majestic from the outside, but they also help create space inside. After all, with the dome doing the "heavy lifting," there's no need for lots of beams or columns to clutter up the space. For more than 1,300 years, the ancient Pantheon in Rome was the largest dome in the world. It lost this title when the Duomo was built in Florence.

Water from the Sun

YOU WILL NEED

- Spade
- Plastic sheet about 3 square feet (0.3 sq m)
- Old coffee mug
- 4 bricks or large stones
- 2 friends

We'll put the "adult needed" warning right up front in this experiment—you'll need an adult's permission to dig a hole in the garden. It can't be just anywhere—you want this hole to catch the most sunlight. After all, you're collecting water from the Sun! Let science explain the magic.

1

Find a spot in the garden that gets a lot of sunlight, but doesn't have flowers already growing there.

2

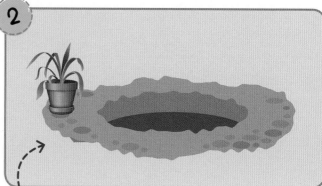

Ask an adult to dig a circular hole, about 20 inches (50 cm) across and 12 inches (30 cm) deep. Keep the dug-up soil near the hole.

3

Set the mug at the bottom of the hole, in the middle.

4

Lay the plastic sheet across the hole. The hole should be at the center of the sheet.

5

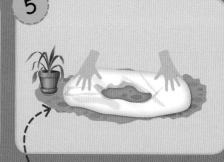

Ask your friends to press down on the corners of the sheet. Carefully scoop the dug-up soil onto the center of the sheet, directly above the mug.

6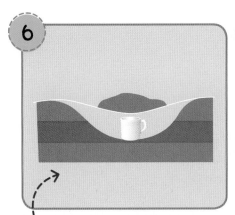

Stop adding soil when the plastic is almost, but not quite, touching the mug.

7

Place a brick on each corner of the sheet.

8

Leave the hole for three hours. Then, carefully remove the bricks and sheet — the mug will contain water!

HOW DOES iT WORK?

You've just demonstrated condensation, a change of matter that occurs when a gas becomes a liquid. Water vapor (the gas form of water) becomes liquid water as it condenses. If it cools suddenly, drops of water form. That's what happens when the warm air finds the cooler, inside surface of the plastic. Drops of water form on that side. And because you weighed down the middle of the sheet, the drops flow down, gather at the lowest point of the sheet, and drip into the mug.

TOP TiP!

It's best to do this experiment on a sunny day to make sure there's a clash of temperatures.

Continued ➡

Make sure the adult helping you doesn't dig through the roots of any plants!

TOP TIP!

When placing the bricks or stones on the sheet, make sure the sheet doesn't slip and touch the mug.

REAL-LIFE SCIENCE

In addition to being dependent on changes in temperature, condensation needs a surface where the liquid can form. You've probably seen this happen on a glass holding a chilled drink, or on the inside of a car window. Tiny bits of dust are constantly floating around in the atmosphere. Water vapor condenses on these dusty flecks to form rain!

WHAT HAPPENS IF...?

The hole in the ground is important in this experiment, and it's all down to the temperature of the air. Even a small hole like this one has cooler air than outside—think of it as a tiny cave. You've found a way to cool the air on one side of the sheet. What would happen if the mug rested on the lawn, with the plastic above it?

Glossary

air pressure The constant pressing of air on everything it touches.

density The amount of mass something has in relation to its volume (or space that it takes up).

friction The force that causes a moving object to slow down.

gas A substance that can expand to fill any shape.

liquid A substance that flows freely but keeps the same volume.

molecule The smallest unit of a substance, such as oxygen, that has all the properties of that substance.

predict To say what will happen in the future or as a result of an action.

solid A substance that is firm with a shape that stays the same.

vapor Tiny particles of a substance spread out in the air.

volume The amount of space a substance takes up inside a container.

Further Information

Books to read

100 Steps for Science: Why it works and how it happened by Lisa Jane Gillespie and Yukai Du (Wide Eyed Editions, 2017)

Mind Webs: Materials by Anna Claybourne (Wayland, 2015)

Whizzy Science: Make it Change by Anna Claybourne (Wayland, 2014)

Websites

http://www.dkfindout.com/us/science/materials/
Learn more about materials at this marvelous site!

https://www.education.com/activity/chemistry/
Check out this site for awesome chemistry activities.

http://www.strangematterexhibit.com/whatis.html
Find cool material facts at this fun site.

Publisher's note to educators and parents: Our editors have carefully reviewed these websites to ensure that they are suitable for students. Many websites change frequently, however, and we cannot guarantee that a site's future contents will continue to meet our high standards of quality and educational value. Be advised that students should be closely supervised whenever they access the Internet.

Index

A

acids 21, 23, 25
air pressure 11, 12, 13

B

barometer 11
bases 21
Bernoulli's Principle 19
buildings 27

C

candle 6, 7, 14, 15
capillary action 7
car 23
carbon dioxide 17, 21, 23
condensation 29, 30
crystals 10

D

density 5
diving 17

F

fluid 18, 19
friction 15

G

gas 7, 13, 17, 19, 21, 22,
    23, 29

H

Henry's Law 17
hovercraft 15

L

liquid 7, 17, 19, 21, 25,
    29, 30

M

molecules 25

O

oil 4, 5, 6, 7

P

plane 19
plants 7

S

salt 4, 5, 8, 10
solid 7, 21, 25
solution 10
states of matter 7, 13
surface tension 15

V

vapor 7, 29, 30

W

water 4, 5, 7, 8, 10, 14, 15,
    17, 18, 23, 28, 29
wax 5
weather 12, 13

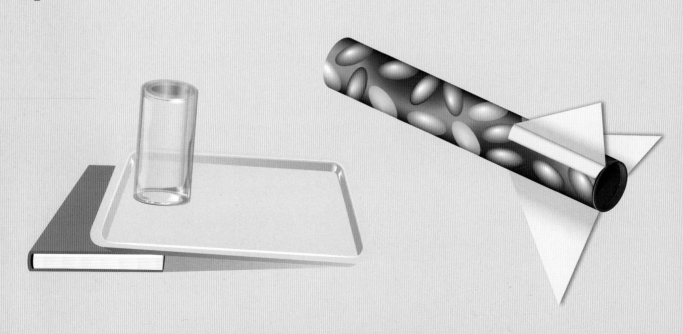